12-10-08

D1469920

RESORT

SHERMAN AVENUE

LIBRARY

CITY HALL

TUBBS HILL

MUDGY & MILLIE

WRITTEN BY
Susan Nipp

ILLUSTRATED BY
Charles Reasoner

Eastern Washington University Press

Printed in China.
Type design by Liz Lester.
"Mudgy & Millie" is a registered trademark of Susan Nipp and Charles Reasoner.

13   12   11   10   09   08   5   4   3   2   1

All royalties from the sale of this book support the Coeur d'Alene Public Library
Foundation. To learn more about Mudgy and Millie, go to www.mudgyandmillie.com.

LIBRARY OF CONGRESS CATALOGING-IN-PUBLICATION DATA

Nipp, Susan Hagen.
      Mudgy and Millie / Susan Hagen Nipp ; with illustrations by Charles
Reasoner.
            p.   cm.
      Summary: When Mudgy Moose suggests playing hide-and-seek, his
friend Millie Mouse finds a hiding place so good that Mudgy trudges all
through Coeur d'Alene, Idaho, looking for her and wondering why people
keep giggling at him.
      ISBN 978-1-59766-042-6 (alk. paper)
      [1. Hide-and-seek—Fiction. 2. Moose—Fiction. 3. Mice—Fiction.
4. Coeur d'Alene (Idaho)—Fiction.] I. Reasoner, Charles, ill. II. Title.
PZ7.N624Mud   2008
[E]—dc22   2008020644

The paper used in this publication meets the minimum requirements of the American
National Standard for Information Services—Permanence of Paper for Printed Library
Materials, ANSI Z39.48—1984.

Eastern Washington University Press
Spokane and Cheney, Washington
http://www.ewu.edu/ewupress/

One sunny, summer day, Mudgy Moose and Millie Mouse were splashing in Coeur d'Alene Lake by Tubbs Hill. Millie, quite drenched from jumping off Mudgy's antlers, said, "Now let's play hide-and-seek!"

Mudgy sloshed out of the water
and excitedly replied, "My favorite
game! Okay! You hide first, Millie."

Mudgy leaned his head on a tall
pine tree, closed his eyes, and
began to loudly count to ten.
"ONE, TWO, THREE . . ."

Millie Mouse had a clever idea. She smiled
to herself as she quietly climbed up the
pine tree." . . . FOUR, FIVE, SIX . . ."

Ever so slowly, Millie
crept into Mudgy's antlers,
" . . . SEVEN, EIGHT . . ."
and gently snuggled down.

Mudgy Moose finished counting,
" . . . NINE, TEN," and shouted,
"Here I come, ready or not!"

Then Mudgy began to look for Millie.
He searched behind rocks and under
bushes. He looked up in the green
fir trees and down around the colorful
wildflowers. But Mudgy couldn't
find Millie anywhere.

"Perhaps she's on the trail. Or maybe she went into town to hide," he thought. "I'll go look."

Millie giggled to herself as she wrapped her tail around Mudgy's antlers and held on for the bumpy ride. Mudgy Moose eagerly trotted down the path through the forest to Coeur d'Alene.

Some hikers were just starting up the trail. Mudgy stopped and asked, "Have you seen Millie Mouse hiding on the trail?" Millie peeked from behind Mudgy's antlers and quietly put her finger to her mouth. "Shhhhh."

The hikers laughed and said, "No, Millie isn't hiding on the trail." Mudgy wondered why they were laughing. "Thank you anyway," he said, and he continued on his way.

Mudgy thought, "Millie loves books.
Maybe she's hiding in the library."
He skipped down the sidewalk
to go find out.

Mudgy looked through the window into the library.

The librarian saw him and came out. Mudgy asked, "Have you seen Millie Mouse hiding in the library?" Millie peeked from behind Mudgy's antlers. "Shhhhh."

The librarian chuckled and said, "No, Millie isn't hiding in the library." Mudgy wondered why she was chuckling. "Thank you anyway," he said, and he continued on his way.

"Hmmm, where should I look next?" thought Mudgy. "Millie loves people and stores and cars and lights and restaurants. Maybe she's hiding somewhere downtown."

Mudgy strolled down the street looking in all directions. He saw some shoppers and asked, "Have you seen Millie Mouse hiding downtown?"

Millie peeked from behind Mudgy's antlers. "Shhhhh."

The shoppers grinned and one little voice said, "No, Millie isn't hiding downtown." Mudgy wondered why they were grinning. "Thank you anyway," he said, and he continued on his way.

Mudgy was puzzled. Where could Millie be?
He needed to think so he slowly walked
around the boardwalk. He thought and
thought. Boats were coming and going
but he didn't even notice.

Suddenly Mudgy stopped. He thought of one more place.
Millie peered over his antlers, wondering where they would go next.

"Millie loves to play at the playground," Mudgy thought.
"Maybe she's hiding in City Park."

Deciding that must be the place, Mudgy galloped to the park to begin his search.

Mudgy went straight
to the playground.
He looked down from
the tall tower,
peered over the
wobbly bridge,
and peeked under
the tunnel slide.

Mudgy saw some children playing. He asked, "Have you seen Millie Mouse hiding in the park?"

Millie peeked from behind Mudgy's antlers. "Shhhhh." The children giggled and said, "No, Millie isn't hiding in the park."

Mudgy wondered why they were giggling. "Thank you anyway," he said, but he didn't continue on his way. He was getting tired from all that trotting and skipping and strolling and walking and galloping.

Mudgy found a
grassy spot under some trees,
snuggled down, and fell asleep. When he
began to snore, Millie thought, "Hmmm . . .
This would be a good time for me to play!"
She slowly crept out of Mudgy's antlers
and quietly slipped
to the ground.

Millie scampered
back to the playground.
She balanced on the beam,
tiptoed through the tunnel,

and swung on the swings.

Finally, she scurried up the slide.
"Whee!" she cried as she slid
down with glee.

After all her playing, Millie was now tired, too. Seeing that Mudgy was still asleep, she carefully crept back into his antlers and settled in for a little nap.

When Mudgy woke up, he was very thirsty. He decided to go down to the lake for a drink. He stood up so quickly that he nearly knocked Millie out of his antlers. Suddenly waking up, she held on as Mudgy hiked through the park to Independence Point.

Mudgy stopped at the edge of the water. As he began to lean down toward the lake, he heard someone laughing, and giggling, and chuckling.

He looked to his left.

He looked to his right.

He didn't see anyone.
Millie quickly covered her
mouth to hold back her giggles.

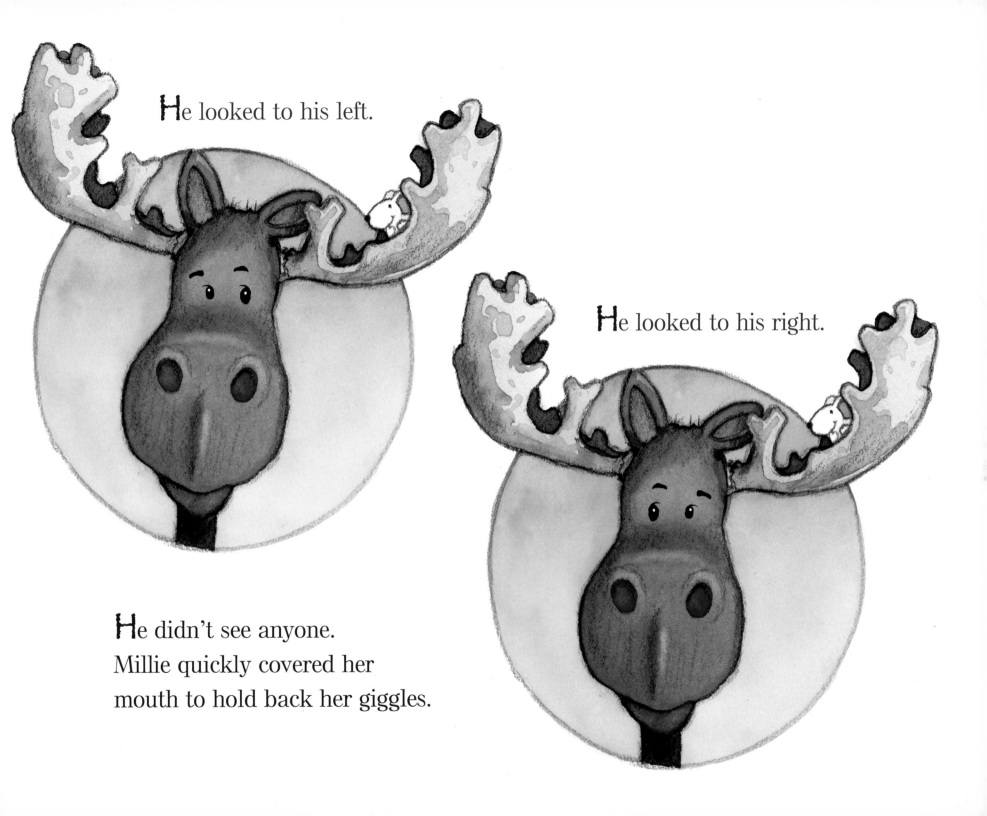

Again Mudgy leaned down to get a drink. As his head neared the water, he saw a strange reflection. He saw his big brown nose. He saw his big brown eyes. He saw his big brown ears.

But, wait! What was that dangling from his big brown antlers? It was Millie Mouse, grinning and hanging on tightly so she wouldn't fall into the water!

Mudgy began to laugh. His body shook and his head shook and his antlers shook.

Millie began to laugh, too. Her body shook and her head shook and her whiskers shook. They both laughed so hard that Millie bounced from Mudgy's antlers onto his big brown nose.

Mudgy looked cross-eyed at Millie. "What a perfect hiding place!" he exclaimed. "It sure was," Millie laughed. "I really fooled you!"

"**W**ell," Mudgy chuckled, "you'd better get ready! Because now . . .

it's MY turn to hide!"

Chuck Reasoner
ILLUSTRATOR

Chuck Reasoner has been creating and illustrating best-selling children's books for nearly thirty years. Chuck's imaginative and fun-filled illustrations are colorful evidence of his belief that reading stimulates a child's future creativity. Chuck brought *Mudgy & Millie* to life in his studio in Taos, New Mexico.

Susan Nipp
AUTHOR

Susan Nipp co-created *Wee Sing*, an award winning series of children's books, CDs, and videos, in 1977. Thirty years later, *Wee Sing* has sold millions of copies, entertaining children, parents, and teachers throughout the world. Susan had the inspiration for *Mudgy & Millie* while hiking through the forest near her home overlooking Coeur d'Alene, Idaho.

Terry Lee
SCULPTOR

Terry Lee is an internationally recognized sculptor and painter, especially known for his colorful wildlife oils and large bronzes. His work is found in numerous galleries and collections throughout the country. Terry has given dimension to *Mudgy & Millie* in the form of five life-size bronze sculptures that are now found along the Mudgy Moose Trail in Coeur d'Alene, Idaho, Terry's hometown.

Follow the Mudgy Moose Trail in Coeur d'Alene, Idaho, and discover five full-size bronze statues of Mudgy and Millie created by artist Terry Lee.

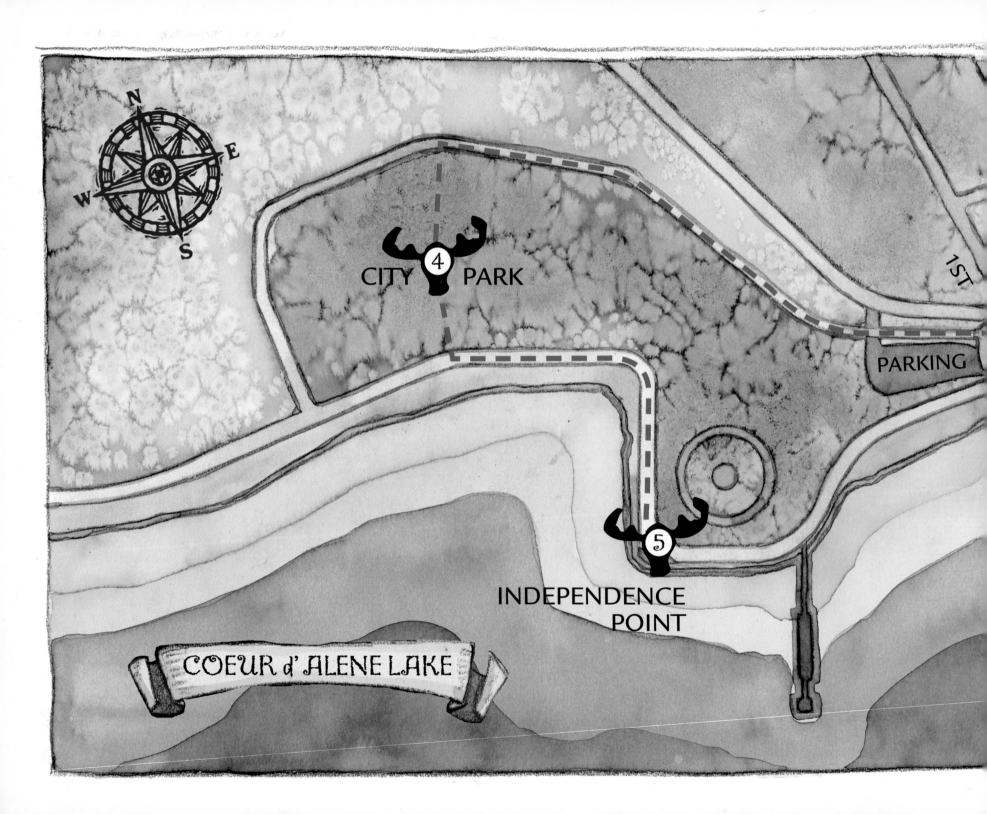